DOG vs. ULTRA DOG

Story by **Troy Wilson**

Art by **Clayton Hanmer**

Owlkids Books

Tuffy loved Tim.

And Tim loved Tuffy.

Tim watched Ultra Dog shows.
He read Ultra Dog books. Played
Ultra Dog video games. Skated
on an Ultra Dog board, and
splashed in an Ultra Dog pool.
Wore Ultra Dog capes, Ultra
Dog caps, and Ultra Dog—

What if Bosworth is a teeny-tiny bit right?

I'll never be the ultra-est dog in the universe—but I bet I can be the ultra-est at obedience!

So when Tim said, "Shake a paw," Tuffy shook all four.

When Tim said, "Fetch the stick," he fetched a stack.

And when Tim said, "Roll over," he rolled and rolled and rooooooolled.

Bosworth might be right. But maybe I can be the ultra-est at chores.

So he cleaned Tim's room.

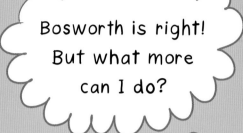

Bosworth is right! But what more can I do?

Can I be... the ultra-est at love?

So he kissed.

Tuffy knew he couldn't fly like Ultra Dog. And try as he might, he couldn't fly like anything else, either.

But then...

To Shannon Riggs,
Ricardo Lane, and
their well-loved
dogs —T.W.

To all my pets,
past and present...
may you always
be Ultra —C.H.

Owlkids Books acknowledges the financial support of the Canada Council for the Arts, the Ontario Arts Council, the Government of Canada through the Canada Book Fund (CBF) and the Government of Ontario through the Ontario Media Development Corporation's Book Initiative for our publishing activities.

Published in Canada by
Owlkids Books Inc.
1 Eglinton Avenue East
Toronto, ON M4P 3A1

Published in the United States by
Owlkids Books Inc.
1700 Fourth Street
Berkeley, CA 94710

Library of Congress Control Number: 2018946403

Library and Archives Canada Cataloguing in Publication

Wilson, Troy, 1970-, author
    Dog vs. Ultra Dog / written by Troy Wilson ; illustrated by Clayton Hanmer.

ISBN 978-1-77147-318-7 (hardcover)
    I. Hanmer, Clayton, 1978-, illustrator II. Title. III. Title: Dog versus Ultra Dog

PS8645.I48D63 2019   jC813'.6   C2018-903747-4

Edited by Debbie Rogosin | Designed by Alisa Baldwin

Manufactured in Dongguan, China, in October 2018, by Toppan Leefung Packaging & Printing (Dongguan) Co., Ltd.
Job #BAYDC60

A   B   C   D   E   F

ONTARIO ARTS COUNCIL
CONSEIL DES ARTS DE L'ONTARIO
an Ontario government agency
un organisme du gouvernement de l'Ontario

Canada Council   Conseil des Arts
for the Arts   du Canada

Canada

OWL kids   Publisher of Chirp, Chickadee and OWL
www.owlkidsbooks.com

Owlkids Books is a division of   Bayard CANADA